Tiger's Bedtime

By Stephanie Calmenson
Illustrated by Tom Cooke

A GOLDEN BOOK • NEW YORK
Western Publishing Company, Inc., Racine, Wisconsin 53404

 ISBN: 0-307-10053-7/ISBN: 0-307-68753-8 (lib. bdg.) C D E F G H I J

It was Tiger's bedtime. He washed his face and brushed his teeth.

Then his mommy came to tuck him in.

"I'm not sleepy," Tiger said.

"But you've had such a busy day," said Mrs. Tiger. "Why don't you tell me what you did?"

Tiger thought about his day.

"First I visited Monkey," Tiger said. "We did tricks to make her baby brother laugh."

"That's nice," said Mrs. Tiger.

"Then I played hide-and-seek with Elephant and Lion," Tiger said. "They couldn't find *me*!"

"I know what you did next," said Tiger's mommy. "You came home for lunch. You had two peanut butter sandwiches."

"Mmm-hmm," said Tiger. "I like peanut butter sandwiches!"

"Then what did you do?" asked Mrs. Tiger.

"I went swimming with Alligator. The water was c-c-cold!" said Tiger.

"Oh, w-w-was it?" said Mrs. Tiger.

"Yes," Tiger said. "So we went back to Alligator's house. We got warm and dry in the sun."

"Then Alligator's mommy helped us bake shape cookies to have with our milk," Tiger said.

"After that, you came home and played in your room," said Mrs. Tiger.

"Then you had your supper and a bath," she said.

"And here I am!" said Tiger.

"Are you sure you're not sleepy?" asked Mrs. Tiger.

"Well, maybe just a little," Tiger said.

“Sweet dreams,” said Tiger’s mommy.

But Tiger didn’t hear her. He had fallen fast asleep.